# North Country Christmas

*The Twins Happy Tales!*

*Shelley Gill* (signature)

*1996*

Story concept by Julie Kemper and Michael Meade

Written by SHELLEY GILL       Illustrated by SHANNON CARTWRIGHT

# North Country Christmas

**Text Copyright 1992**
**Shelley Gill, Julie Kemper**
**and Michael Meade**
**Illustration copyright 1992**
**Shannon Cartwright**
**Edited by Deborah Tobola**

ISBN 0-934007-14-4 paper
ISBN 0-934007-18-7 cloth
Library of Congress #: 92-090776
Printed in the United States
First Edition 1992

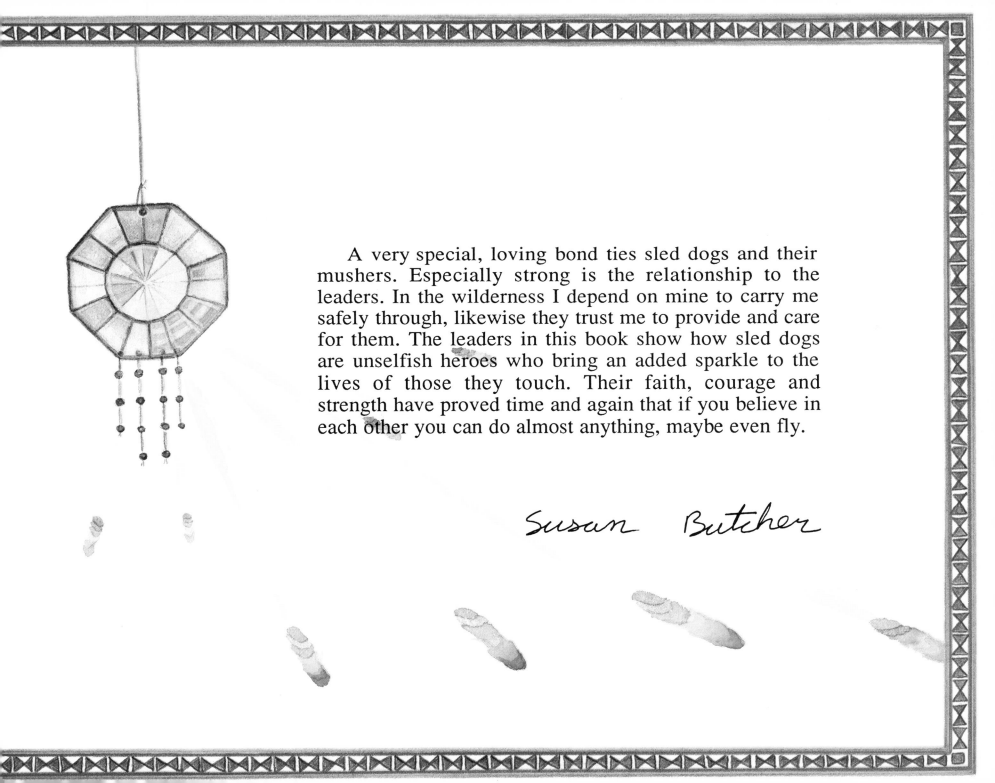

A very special, loving bond ties sled dogs and their mushers. Especially strong is the relationship to the leaders. In the wilderness I depend on mine to carry me safely through, likewise they trust me to provide and care for them. The leaders in this book show how sled dogs are unselfish heroes who bring an added sparkle to the lives of those they touch. Their faith, courage and strength have proved time and again that if you believe in each other you can do almost anything, maybe even fly.

*Susan Butcher*

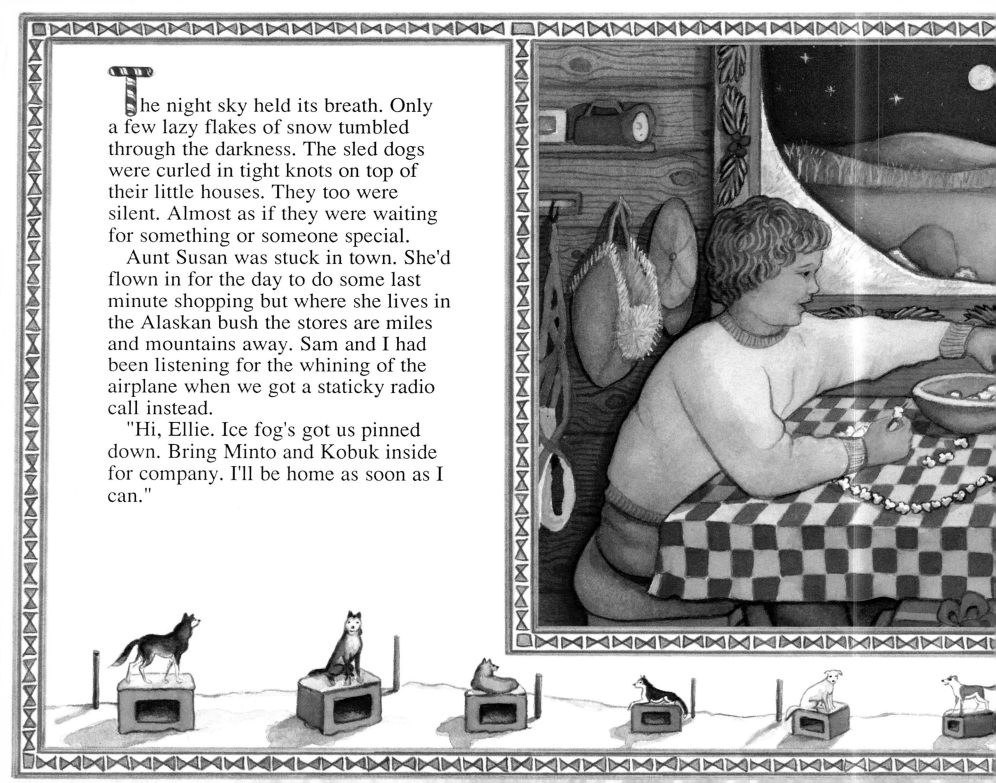

The night sky held its breath. Only a few lazy flakes of snow tumbled through the darkness. The sled dogs were curled in tight knots on top of their little houses. They too were silent. Almost as if they were waiting for something or someone special.

Aunt Susan was stuck in town. She'd flown in for the day to do some last minute shopping but where she lives in the Alaskan bush the stores are miles and mountains away. Sam and I had been listening for the whining of the airplane when we got a staticky radio call instead.

"Hi, Ellie. Ice fog's got us pinned down. Bring Minto and Kobuk inside for company. I'll be home as soon as I can."

In the silence I wriggled into my parka and shoved my hands in woolly mittens. The clink of the door's metal latch echoed as I stepped into the cold. Moonlight washed through the dog yard and licked around the edges of the porch. In the east, the Northern Lights divided the sky with a thin line of green and gold.

I unhooked Kobuk first, then Minto. Kobuk ran straight for the door but Minto twirled around me in happy circles, her breath leaving little puffs of frost in the soft light.

Sam's face was framed in the window. We both watched as the Northern Lights pulsed and swayed in wider and wider streaks of pink and green and gold.

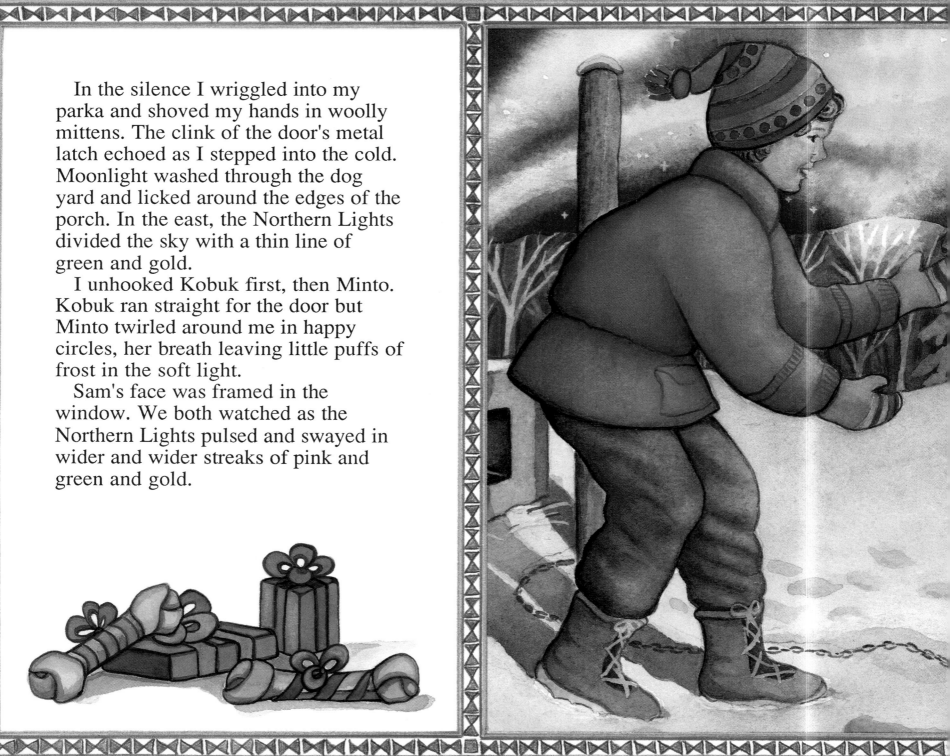

Inside Minto curled up on a faded red quilt. Sam sank into his chair.

"Someone told me the Northern Lights are really moonlight reflected off icebergs drifting out at sea," Sam said as he watched me throw another log in the stove.

"Well, don't believe everything you hear. They're caused by explosions on the sun." I knew this because our sixth grade class studied the aurora borealis, which is the real name for the Northern Lights. But Sam was just a fourth grader, so he didn't know much of anything yet.

Sam leaned forward to pick up a book then surprised me by reading out loud.

And it
on Chri
crea
voi

came to be that
tmas Eve all the
ures lifted their
es and spoke to
one another in
peace...

He looked up. "Do you believe that, Ellie?"

I slowly shook my head. "I dunno. I'd like to, I guess. Maybe the french poodles even speak French," I giggled. "It sure would be a neat Christmas present if old Minto could talk, huh?" Sam laughed and we both headed for bed.

Upstairs our room was bright with moonlight. I warmed under the weight of the covers and listened as the hiss and spit of the fire slipped me into sleep.

A sharp knock at the cabin door snapped me awake. Sam fumbled with the kerosene light. Funny, the dogs hadn't barked. Even Minto was quiet as she sat, her head cocked toward the door.

Sam cautiously slid back the bolt. An old man stood in the moonlight. Dark eyes shone from wrinkled brown skin. A wisp of sparse white whiskers brushed against the most beautiful parka I had ever seen. His mittens and mukluks were trimmed in soft fur and beaded and tied with gold braid. He smiled and nodded his hello.

"My name's Nick. I know I'm a bit early but I need Susan's help."

"She's not here," I said quickly. "We were expecting you for Christmas dinner tomorrow night."

"Yep." As Nick spoke he rubbed Minto's ears. First one, then the other. "I need to borrow some dogs. My team's all worn out. We've been traveling since dawn and I still have one more stop to make."

"Sure," said Sam, before I could argue.

"Wait. You gotta let us come too," I added. "We're responsible for the dogs when Susan's gone."

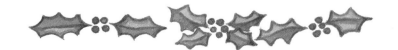

"You bet!" said Nick. "I'd enjoy the company."

Sam struggled into his coat and wind pants while I grabbed my gear. By the time my boots were laced Nick had the dogs in harness.

"Hey Nick. Minto can't lead. She's too old."

"Don't worry about her," he said as he fastened Kobuk and Pirate's necklines. "Minto's a champ."

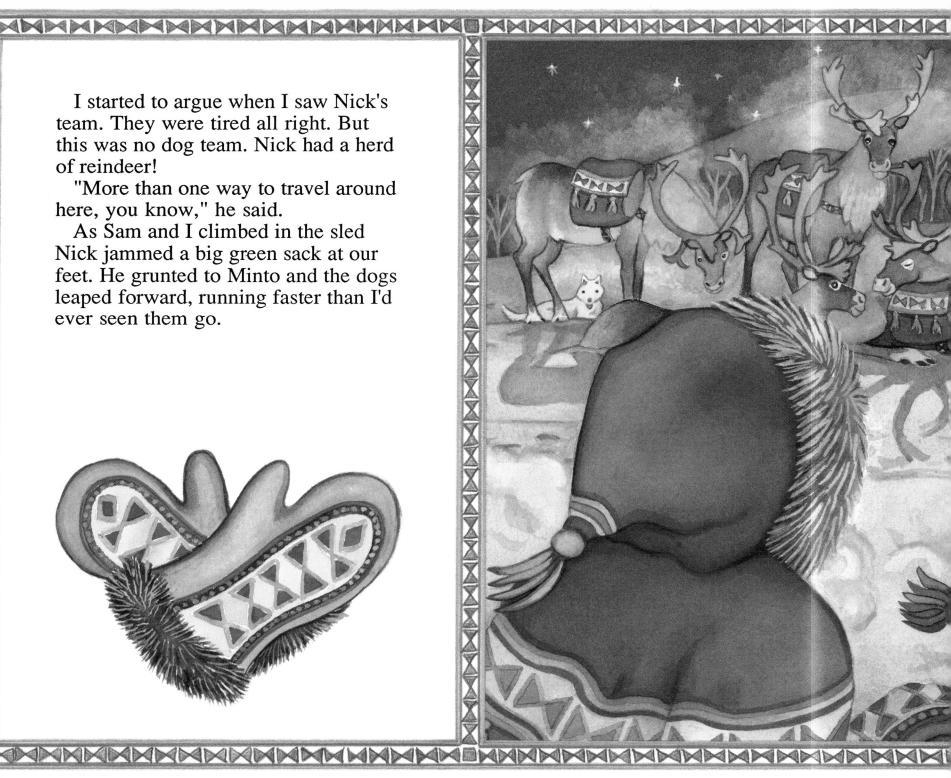

I started to argue when I saw Nick's team. They were tired all right. But this was no dog team. Nick had a herd of reindeer!

"More than one way to travel around here, you know," he said.

As Sam and I climbed in the sled Nick jammed a big green sack at our feet. He grunted to Minto and the dogs leaped forward, running faster than I'd ever seen them go.

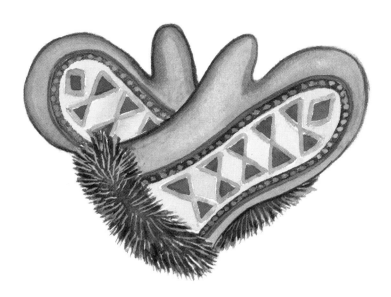

We skimmed over the snow, our sled runners whispering, the dogs panting and our breath making crystal clouds that covered our faces with a film of frost.

The blue face of the moon beckoned us closer and we went faster and faster until it seemed we would fly.

"Whoa!" Nick called to the dogs. They slowed and stopped on a low ridge above a small village. A smoky orange glow encircled the worn wooden houses.

"Where are we?" I asked, breathless.

"Kikuyat."

"But what are we doing here?" asked Sam.

"Helping out," Nick said as he pulled his sack from the sled. "This village is having hard times. So we've come to share some Christmas magic." From the big sack he pulled two smaller ones and handed them to us.

"The people of Kikuyat need food to eat," he said. He showed us what was inside his sack. Jars of ripe berries and jam, smoked fish and spiced meat. "But people need more than just meat for the body. We brought some food for the spirit too."

He pointed to our sacks. I reached inside and pulled out a beautiful glass crystal that hung from a piece of blue silk. There were dozens inside and each was different and wonderful.

"Oooh," Sam and I sighed.

"They remind me of snowflakes," Nick whispered. "The People have many names for the snow that covers their land. My favorite is 'saviguk'. It means 'ice crystals floating in the air'. Tomorrow when the sun rises and shines through these crystals the village of Kikuyat will be painted in rainbows."

Nick handed us each a sack. "Hang 'em up then meet back here. And hurry, we don't have much time."

Racing from one small plank house to the next, Sam and I hung the crystals from nails, hooks, fish racks and window frames.

By the time we got back to the sled Nick and the dogs were ready.

"I don't want to go!" cried Sam. "Let's stay and watch the sun rise."

"We can't," I said. "It won't be up until noon." But we could imagine the rainbow of colors scattered across the fresh snow. "I guess we'll never know what they look like." Reluctantly we climbed into the sled.

Nick stepped onto the runners and Minto surged ahead. "Hold on!" he shouted and we grabbed the sides of the sled.

As we flew up the trail the sky around us burst into spectacular color. We could taste the tart greens, pinks and yellows and hear the singing of the stars as we shot straight ahead into the heart of the Northern Lights.

We rode a carousel of colors, shapes and sounds. Tiny snowflakes tumbled by, cartwheeling on smooth sapphire spears. Giant lacey flakes bobbed and hummed in the moon's blue glow. I leaned into a rainbow of pink streaked ice that whirled and swirled like waves cresting in a wild sea. Yellow almost swallowed me. Green rode behind us nipping at the runners of our sled.

I could see Sam's shining eyes. Am I dreaming? I wondered. By tomorrow I would know for sure. If this was real Sam would never stop talking about it.

Moments before midnight we were home. Nick and his reindeer were off again in a flash. "I'll be back in time for dinner," he promised.

Sam waited for me at the door of the cabin. "Aunt Susan will never believe this," he whispered.

I nodded. But just before I followed him inside, I heard a clear, sweet voice say, "Yes she will."

I whirled around to see old Minto, winking at Kobuk beneath the twinkling Christmas sky.